An Insanely Funny
Guided Journal

F·R·I·E·N·D·S
THE TELEVISION SERIES

GUIDE TO
ADULTING

by Samantha Mannis

THUNDER BAY
P·R·E·S·S

San Diego, California

Thunder Bay Press
An imprint of Printers Row Publishing Group
10350 Barnes Canyon Road, Suite 100, San Diego, CA 92121
www.thunderbaybooks.com • mail@thunderbaybooks.com

Published in the United States by Thunder Bay Press
in conjunction with Warner Bros. Global Publishing.

Printers Row Publishing Group is a division of Readerlink Distribution
Services, LLC. Thunder Bay Press is a registered trademark of Readerlink
Distribution Services, LLC.

Correspondence regarding the content of this book should be sent
to Thunder Bay Press, Editorial Department, at the above address.

Publisher: Peter Norton
Associate Publisher: Ana Parker
Senior Developmental Editor: April Graham Farr
Developmental Editor: Diane Cain
Editor: Jessica Matteson
Production Team: Jonathan Lopes, Rusty von Dyl, Beno Chan

Author: Samantha Mannis
Designer: Rosemary Rae

ISBN: 978-1-64517-365-6

Printed in China

24 23 22 21 20   1 2 3 4 5

INTRODUCTION

WHETHER YOU'RE GRADUATING COLLEGE, MOVING TO A NEW CITY, OR GOING THROUGH YOUR FIRST (OR FIFTIETH) BREAKUP, ADULTING ISN'T ALL AVOCADO TOAST AND SUNSHINE—THOUGH YOUR SOCIAL MEDIA FEED MAY BEG TO DIFFER.

Now that you're an adult, you have to do "adult things." This may include finding a job, scheduling your own doctor's appointments, learning to cook food that doesn't come in a frozen package, and handling the many highs and lows of life in between.

Right now these tasks may seem daunting, especially when all you really want to do is curl up in a ball on your couch, binge all ten seasons of *Friends* with your cat who doesn't even like you, and go back to a time where the only DMs you had to worry about were from someone named GLITTERGURL92.

It makes sense! *Friends* just has a way of understanding all of our adulting woes. Whether you grew up watching the show or are part of the new generation finding comfort in surveying the lives of twentysomething New Yorkers, look around—we're all now adults, and it's time we started acting like it. I mean, if we have to. Wait, do we actually have to?

Friends Guide To Adulting is here to get you through the peaks and valleys of adulting, with advice from our six favorite friends, Rachel, Monica, Phoebe, Chandler, Joey, and Ross.

Ever wondered what tips Chandler would give on how to get through the work day? Maybe you're curious about how to become a pro at cleaning like Monica.

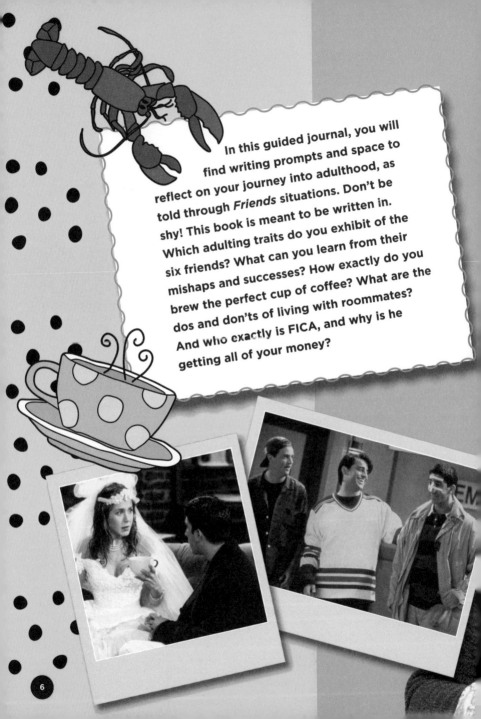

In this guided journal, you will find writing prompts and space to reflect on your journey into adulthood, as told through *Friends* situations. Don't be shy! This book is meant to be written in. Which adulting traits do you exhibit of the six friends? What can you learn from their mishaps and successes? How exactly do you brew the perfect cup of coffee? What are the dos and don'ts of living with roommates? And who exactly is FICA, and why is he getting all of your money?

Even if no one told you life was gonna be this way, adulting can be a really magical time.

Take a seat on your comfy orange couch at your favorite coffee shop (doesn't everyone have one of those?) and take the time to think about what it means to be an adult. With all the fill-ins, flashbacks, and advice from your favorite friends, you're sure to do a little adulting by the end of this book!

ROOMMATES

For many of us, *Friends* was the first peek into life with a roommate. But as much as you may love the idea of cohabiting with people like Rachel, Monica, Phoebe, Joey, Chandler, and Ross, you may find yourself face to face with the Eddie of roommates. Whether you're starting college with a brand-new roommate or are moving into your first apartment with a couple of your best buddies, take a few lessons from the six friends so you can start off on the right foot and achieve total roomie goals.

Roommate Dos and Don'ts!

DOS
- ✓ Do wear oven mitts when making fajitas.
- ✓ Do make a living-room fort with your roommate.
- ✓ Do have a drink in a wedding dress as a pick-me-up.
- ✓ Do spend the day in a box to show your roommate how sorry you are.
- ✓ Do the dirty dishes. Just do them.

DON'TS
- ✓ Don't forget to pivot on moving day.
- ✓ Don't confuse your phone number for your phone bill.
- ✓ Don't look for a potential roommate at the grocery store.
- ✓ Don't throw a pizza box down the trash chute.
- ✓ Don't think mini muffins will get you the apartment of your dreams.

pivot!

IT'S HARD TO IMAGINE THE SIX FRIENDS WITHOUT CENTRAL PERK. But if you have spent any amount of time adulting, you'll begin to realize why the gang was always hanging out around that cozy coffee house.

Coffee is an essential tool to mastering complete adult harmony. Once you have real-world responsibilities, plus have the added stress of deadlines and aging (gross), you suddenly start to crave more caffeine (and couch time). Soon you'll start to see the patterns, as life begins to revolve more and more around coffee: coffee breaks, coffee dates, coffee pods, coffee art (this will look great on the 'Gram!).

So while you take some time to ponder the importance of caffeine in your life, enjoy this introduction to the many ways you can infuse coffee into your day and your veins. Seriously, you may need an IV drip at some point; it works miracles.

JOEY DOESN'T SHARE FOOD: COFFEE!

HOW TO DRINK COFFEE THE FRIENDS WAY

STEP ONE: Head to Central Perk to meet up with your friends who are also heading to Central Perk at the exact same time.

STEP TWO: Grab the couch that is always available for you and your group.

STEP THREE: Order coffee.

STEP FOUR: Drink coffee.

STEP FIVE: Order more coffee and get Chandler to pay for it.

STEP SIX: Ignore Gunther's presence entirely.

How to Drink Coffee IRL

Step 1: Get coffee pod.
Step 2: Insert pod...somewhere.
Step 3: Coffee slithers out.
Step 4: Rush to put mug underneath (you forgot mug).
Step 5: Drink miserable watery slush in your cubicle.
Step 6: Realize you took grumpy Jeff from Accounting's mug and go hide.
Step 7: Remind yourself not to repeat.
Step 8: Take home mug.

BONUS: How to Brew Coffee the Old-School Way

- Measure your water in the pot then transfer it to the machine.
- Measure your coffee grounds and add them to the machine (don't forget a filter!).
- Use about one to two tablespoons of ground coffee for every six ounces of water. You can adjust the amount of coffee to your taste.
- Brew!
- Remove from heat and pour into big mug or to-go cup.

I'm GONNA go GET one OF THOSE JOB THINGS.

—RACHEL GREEN

BAD ADULTING HABITS

- ☐ Lazy roommate
- ☐ Jealous ex-girlfriend
- ☐ Bad driver
- ☐ Cannot make coffee (and works at a coffeehouse)
- ☐ Former high-school bully
- ☐ Messy
- ☐ Cannot get ready on time
- ☐ No cooking skills whatsoever

GOOD ADULTING HABITS

- ☐ Trendsetter
- ☐ Hair trailblazer
- ☐ Loyal
- ☐ Goes after what she wants
- ☐ Isn't afraid to try new things
- ☐ Brave
- ☐ Supportive friend
- ☐ Loving mother

RACHEL'S CHECKLIST

Rachel Green's hair may always be on point, but perfect hair doesn't always make for a perfect life (shocker, right?). Nonetheless, this fashion guru has a lot to teach when it comes to adulting.

Check off each of the good and bad adulting qualities you exhibit in your own life. How alike or different are you from Rachel?

BIG BOOK OF GRIEVANCES: LiFE

REMEMBER WHEN CHANDLER FINDS HECKLES'S BiG BOOK OF GRIEVANCES?

Adulting certainly comes with its own set of complaints, whether it be exorbitant surge pricing (you put up with it because you are lit and you only have a bag of spicy, slightly stale cheesy poofs at home), to low wages (seriously, how can anyone afford to get home to their cheese poofs on that salary?!).

Rather than shut yourself out from the world and collect all of your complaints in a dusty old book, here is a page for you to air your life's grievances so you can continue on without driving yourself absolutely nuts.

GUIDE TO:

LOOKING YOUR BEST

Looking great is crucial to putting your best foot forward in life.

And besides, a good glow-up is also a truly fantastic way to show off and drive your haters crazy. (I see you, Fat Monica.) So feel free to milk both.

If you are looking to post a 10/10 photo on the 'Gram, make sure everything is on point. That means eyebrows on fleek (no botched brow jobs, Joey), the right amount of tan (try "Mississippily" instead of "Mississippi"), and flashing those pearly whites (note: pearly is not the same as glow-in-the-dark with a black light).

Keep in mind that this isn't just about the physical—it's a state of mind. Ultimately, looking your best is about feeling your best, so be confident in what you have to offer, even if your hair just won't cooperate.

"It's the humidity!"

Winners can play through any bad hair day.

Maybe you are like Chandler and can't commit to a relationship (the "Oh. My. God!" does get a little annoying after a while), or your estranged parents are finally meeting face to face at a lousy non-Thanksgiving dinner. Adulting can get overwhelming when these sorts of problems start flying toward you at full speed.

Fill in whatever problem you're facing and then think about how Chandler would handle it. Do you agree? Would you do the same?

What's On Your Mind?

_____

_____

_____

_____

_____

_____

_____

_____

What Would Chandler Do?

_____

_____

_____

_____

_____

_____

_____

"Oh. My. God!"

TRIP DOWN MEMORY LANE:

SCHOOL

Being a full-time person is hard, and it's an understatement to say that life can get a little overwhelming. Sometimes it just gets you thinking: can't I just go back to school and jam on my electric keyboards? Sigh. Alas, if only it were that simple. But luckily you don't have to go back in time just to lay down those tracks.

Take a moment to reflect on the questions below about a younger version of yourself when all of life's problems seemed a little less...adult.

What is your favorite memory from high school?

_____

_____

_____

_____

What were some of your biggest challenges you faced in school?

_____

_____

_____

_____

How have they changed since then?

_____

_____

_____

_____

In what ways have you grown?

_____

_____

_____

_____

TURNING THIRTY

Even if you may technically still be twenty-nine in Guam (nice catch, Rachel), eventually you will have to come to terms with the fact that you are no longer in your youthful twenties. Wake up and smell the coffee, sunshine.

You are officially as old as the jar of organic almond butter in your pantry. But here's the thing: Everyone turns thirty, including all of your friends. Luckily you don't have to get through this milestone alone. So dust off your old cheerleading uniform and get ready to cry into your cake. *This birthday is going to suck!*

Dirty Thirty Dos and Don'ts

✓ Do throw a fun party with all your friends.

✓ Don't get plastered at your birthday bash and reveal all your family secrets.

✓ Do blow out the candles and eat cake.

✓ Don't give your thirty-year-old girlfriend a scooter as a gift. It's tacky, son.

✓ Do practice gratitude for the people and things in your life.

✓ Don't give your friend a stupid birthday card that pokes fun at her age.

✓ Do set exciting, brand-new goals for this brand-new decade.

✓ Don't forget the year you were born and miss your thirtieth birthday altogether (nice going, Pheebs).

FINDING YOUR
Love LOBSTER

Remember when Phoebe tells Ross "She's your lobster" in reference to Rachel? Through this crustacean love story, Phoebe noted that lobsters mate for life, and Ross and Rachel were destined to end up together. Pretty romantic, right? Even if lobsters are the mutant spiders of the ocean.

If you are looking for a partner in love, how can you really tell if that person is your lobster or just a plain old bottom feeder? You can start with clarifying some things for yourself right here and right now.

"She's your lobster!"

Take some time to journal below and reflect on what you are looking for in your love life.

What do you think of Phoebe's take on soul mates? Is it possible for humans to find their "lobster"?

_____

_____

_____

_____

What are some qualities that you think are essential to have in a life partner?

_____

_____

_____

_____

Is finding a lobster in love important to you right now? Maybe you have other priorities (you can have lobsters in other areas of your life as well). If so, what are they?

_____

_____

_____

_____

JOEY'S
• GUIDE TO •
aDULTiNG

1. Always take the time to ask a friend, "HOW you doin'?"

2. If the fridge breaks, eat everything.

3. Don't fall in love with your hot roommates.

4. Maternity pants also make great Thanksgiving pants.

5. Preparing to lose is just as important, especially when you are expecting to win.

6. Don't agree to model for something unless you know exactly what it's for.

7. If it's between your friend and a sandwich, pick your friend.

8. Never waste a perfectly good trifle.

9. It's not what you say, it's the way you say it.

10. Love is based on having and giving... and sharing... and receiving.

11. Don't stress over something if it's a moo point.

12. If you ever find yourself on a game show, think logically (you probably don't put a ghost in coffee)!

13. Try to stop eating before you get the meat sweats.

14. A thesaurus can really up your letter-writing game.

15. Order two plates of fries when you are out on a date. NEVER SHARE FOOD.

16. Don't steal your best friend's girl, and if you do, be prepared to sit in a box and think about what you did.

17. A foosball table is a great substitute for a kitchen table.

18. Don't borrow clothes from your friend without asking first... and always wear underwear.

Sometimes problems arise that you just don't want to deal with.

Maybe you're fighting with your roommate over dirty dishes (be honest, are you Team Rachel or Team Monica on this?) or their lousy taste in furniture.

Even if things aren't going your way, part of being an adult is learning that the only thing you can truly control is the way you react.

WHAT WOULD *Monica* DO?

Fill in an adulting problem you're currently facing and then think about how Monica would handle it. Do you agree? Would you do anything differently?

What's On Your Mind?

_____

_____

_____

_____

_____

_____

_____

_____

What Would Monica Do?

_____

_____

_____

_____

_____

_____

_____

_____

_____

GUIDE TO:

PeTS

Whether you're raising a chick and duck or have a codependent relationship with a white-headed capuchin named Marcel, taking care of a pet is a huge responsibility. You must provide a loving home, keep your buddy out of trouble, and, of course, there is watching TV together (pass the tortilla chips, plz).

Before you take in a new pet, decide if you can care for them. Are you going to co-parent with your roommate? Will you be a single father to a monkey? Or will you sell your mean, exotic, bald cat named Mrs. Whiskerson to Gunther? Then learn all you can from your new pal. There really is so much to learn!

And if you opt out of caring for an animal friend, consider bringing home an enormous decorative dog named Pat. Pats are pets too.

More Pet Pro Tips

✓ Don't let your duck eat your roommate's engagement ring.

✓ You may have to smash your foosball table if your pets get trapped inside.

✓ Chicks don't swim.

✓ Apartment rats are not pets (RIP, Bob).

✓ Some pets really like to dance to music!

✓ A statue makes a wonderful, low-maintenance pet.

✓ A dog can make a great last-minute groomsman (sorry, Ross and Chandler).

THE ONE
WITH
THE LIST

If you're struggling with a conflict at work, at home, or among friends, it can be difficult to gain clarity without taking some time to reflect on the consequences of your actions.

Remember when Ross made a pros-and-cons list before breaking things off with Julie? Although things could've gone a bit differently (ever heard of a password, Chandler?), the list ultimately helped Ross organize his thoughts so he could see that being with Rachel was what he truly wanted.

Of course, no one wants to make any bad decisions, but that is never fully guaranteed. With a list, you can take the time to reflect on the pros and cons so that you don't make any hasty decisions.

DON'T BE SHY. TRY OUT THE SAME LIST TECHNIQUE THAT ROSS USED RIGHT HERE.

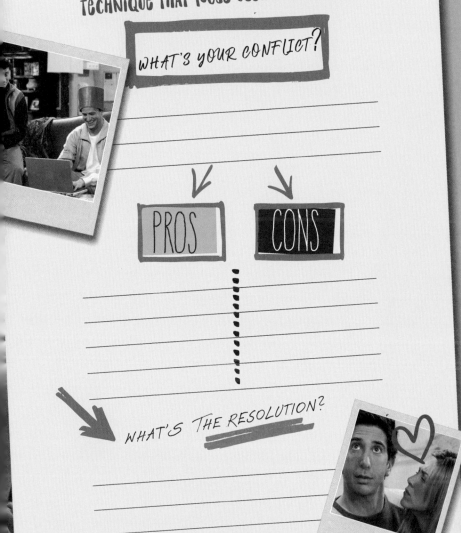

WHAT'S YOUR CONFLICT?

_____
_____
_____

PROS   CONS

_____
_____
_____
_____

WHAT'S THE RESOLUTION?

_____
_____
_____
_____
_____

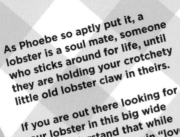

As Phoebe so aptly put it, a lobster is a soul mate, someone who sticks around for life, until they are holding your crotchety little old lobster claw in theirs.

If you are out there looking for your lobster in this big wide world, understand that while you may find a lobster in "love," you can also find your lobster in life. A lobster in life is your life's purpose—something that you were born to do. So strap on your bib because there is definitely more than one lobster coming your way.*

FINDING YOUR
Life LOBSTER

*WARNING: Please do not eat your life partner.

Pick three adjectives that describe what you want for yourself in life. This will lead you one step closer to finding your life lobster.

1 ☐

2 ☐

3 ☐

Jot down a few goals you are looking to achieve in your life.

_____

_____

_____

_____

How will you reach those goals?

_____

_____

_____

_____

_____

"It's a known fact that lobsters fall in love and mate for life. You can actually see old lobster couples, walking around their tank, you know, holding claws."

I TELL YOU, WHEN I ACTUALLY DIE, . . .

SOME PEOPLE ARE GOING TO GET *SERIOUSLY* **HAUNTED.**

—ROSS GELLER

ROSS'S CHECKLIST

A devoted father, brother, and dino-nerd—you gotta give Ross some credit for mastering the art of adulting (and Unagi). However, he really could work on those spray-tan techniques (learn to count, bro).

Check off each of the good and bad adulting qualities you exhibit in your own life. How alike or different are you from Ross?

BAD ADULTING HABITS

☐ Talks about work way too much (have you ever heard of dino/life balance, Ross?)

☐ Serial divorcer

☐ Mansplainer

☐ Jealous tendencies

GOOD ADULTING HABITS

☐ Trendsetter

☐ Good father

☐ Educated

☐ Great job

☐ Generous (he bought Phoebe a bike when he learned that she never had one growing up—pretty nice gesture!)

☐ Stands up for his sibling even if they don't agree on everything

SELF-CARE

If you really want to ace adulting, you will want to level up on your self-care. Although the phrase itself is a little tired, you will find that surrendering to it is much better than being a grumpy, over-worked, sarcastic sack of Funyuns and self-deprivation.

What is self-care? It's caring...for yourself. Like taking a walk, cooking a healthy meal, buying yourself something nice, or simple acts of grooming. Sounds simple, right?

Wrong. Many, many people can be resistant to even the smallest acts of self-care.

Take Chandler, for instance. He really did not want to get into that bubble bath. But with the loving (and forceful) help of Monica and a very cool toy battleship, he settled down into the suds and realized what he was missing.

The value of a self-care routine is priceless! So, like Chandler, get over your toxic fears of some delightful scented candles and soak up all the self-care you can manage. Before you know it, you will be stockpiling fizzy bath bombs, incense, and alone time because it's called being enlightened, dammit.

More Self-Care Pro Tips

- ✓ Hit up your health club for a workout and steam (but watch where you sit)
- ✓ Treat yourself to a massage (just maybe not from your best friend)
- ✓ Indulge in some retail therapy (Rachel knows what's up)
- ✓ Grab a nap partner for some interrupted shut-eye (dibs on Joey!)
- ✓ Take a run in the park (unless you run like Phoebe)

BIG BOOK OF
GRIEVANCES:
Love

From two a.m. texts, to ghosting, to the fact that there are truly not enough decent lobsters to go around, when your love life's DOA, it can be a serious pain in the peach!

But, as Chandler soon discovers, having a big book of grievances shouldn't get in the way of you finding your person.

Take the space below to air your grievances. Maybe you are you fed up with dating or going through a breakup? Maybe you are in a fight with your S.O.? Or maybe love is too darn perfect! Be that as it may, what is bothering you right now in your love life?

UNLIKE JOEY, YOU SHARE FOOD: CHOCOLATE CHIP COOKIES

Having a good chocolate chip cookie recipe in your back pocket is key to surviving adulthood. Imagine all of the horribly inconvenient office potlucks, awkward family gatherings, and lonely Friday nights that you are going to nail.

So here it is: Phoebe's legendary top-secret chocolate chip cookie recipe. Rumor has it, it was passed down from Phoebe's grandmother's grandmother, "Nestle Toulouse"!

If you're ready to take on this enigma of a recipe, then this Buffay family gem is definitely for you. But be sure not to let your cookies burn (Lord knows Phoebe's grandma will for lying about this recipe).

Recipe Preparation

STEP ONE: Lose your grandma's secret cookie recipe.

STEP TWO: Find one last cookie in your fridge.

STEP THREE: Spend your entire weekend with your best friend playing cookie sleuth. Eleven batches of cookies should do the trick.

STEP FOUR: Realize that your grandmother is Satan.

STEP FIVE: Follow this recipe.

BUFFAY FAMILY RECIPE

2 ¼ cups all-purpose flour
1 teaspoon baking soda
1 teaspoon salt
1 cup butter (2 sticks), softened
¾ cup granulated sugar
¾ cup packed brown sugar
1 teaspoon vanilla extract
2 large eggs
2 cups/12 ounces semisweet chocolate chips
1 cup chopped nuts (optional)

Instructions

1. Heat oven to 375. Combine flour, baking soda, and salt in small bowl. Beat butter, granulated sugar, brown sugar, and vanilla extract in large mixing bowl until creamy. Add eggs, one at a time, beating well after each addition. Gradually beat in flour mixture. Stir in chocolate chips and nuts, if using. Drop by rounded tablespoon onto ungreased baking sheets.

2. Bake for 9 to 11 minutes or until golden brown. Cool on baking sheets for 2 minutes; move to wire racks to cool completely.

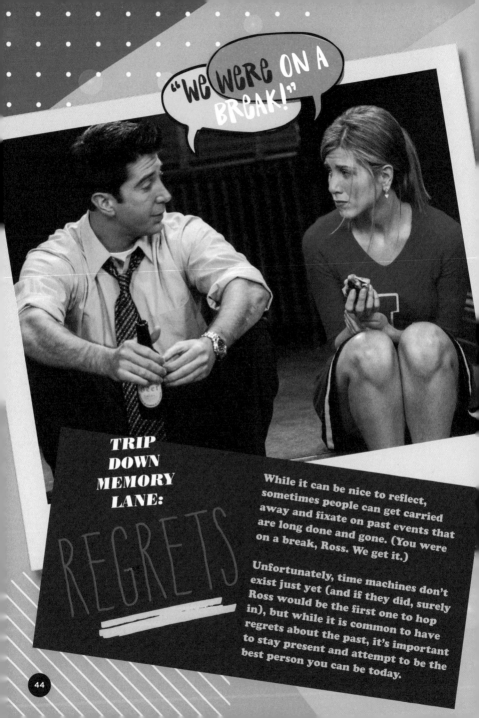

"WE WERE ON A BREAK!"

TRIP DOWN MEMORY LANE:

REGRETS

While it can be nice to reflect, sometimes people can get carried away and fixate on past events that are long done and gone. (You were on a break, Ross. We get it.)

Unfortunately, time machines don't exist just yet (and if they did, surely Ross would be the first one to hop in), but while it is common to have regrets about the past, it's important to stay present and attempt to be the best person you can be today.

Take some time to reflect on the questions below and evaluate your past self whether it be in life, love, or career!

Do you have any regretful events in your past that you wish had gone differently?

_____

_____

_____

_____

_____

Write down a few things that you want to achieve this year.

_____

_____

_____

_____

Moving forward, how can you be the person that you want to be today? (If you are a shoe, and you'd rather be a purse, how can you be that purse?)

_____

_____

_____

_____

RACHEL'S
• GUIDE TO •
aDULTiNG

1. Fake it until you make it—and that includes making coffee.

2. Retail therapy is a thing.

3. It is okay to work a job you hate in pursuit of a life you love.

4. Dating your coworker is not a good idea, even if he is super cute.

5. If you can do laundry, there is nothing you can't do.

6. "The customer is always right, a smile goes a long way, and if anyone is ever rude to you: sneeze muffin."

7. Know when you shouldn't be allowed to make decisions anymore.

8. Read all recipes very carefully, especially when you are in charge of dessert!

9. Get off the plane. It may be the best decision of your life.

10. Never pay $1,000 for a cat. Especially when the cat is bald and you are broke.

11. Everything you need to know is in that first kiss.

12. When you ask someone out on a date, make sure you actually get to go on it.

13. Get closure before you start dating again.

14. A good haircut can do wonders for the soul.

15. It's never too late to tell someone you love them.

16. Don't kiss your boss on a job interview. Or ever.

AGE GAPS

They say age is just
a number, but
you know that
is complete and
utter bull.

Age matters.
When it comes
to you and your
dating life, you
gotta do you,
honey—but if
you are dating
someone who
is old enough
to remember
you peeing in
their pool or
young enough

to be going to sleepaway camp, you may have gotten yourself into a little bit of an awkward situation. Remember when Ross dated his student Elizabeth? They made a cute couple, but after a while it was pretty clear they were in two very different places of life. It was not going to work, and that was only made clearer to Ross when Elizabeth chucked a water balloon at him.

But while lots of couples with age gaps don't work out, others can. Even if you may be subject to some judgment from family and friends and lots of lots of age-related jokes, don't let that scare you away. Sometimes you can find love in the most unexpected places. So, if the relationship fits, wear it. What's a few years in the long run?

WHAT WOULD *phoebe* DO?

Unfortunately, challenging issues can pop up in your life at times when you just can't even.

Maybe your boyfriend moved to Minsk or your apartment unexpectedly burned down. But, in the face of adversity, you can always ask yourself, "What would Phoebe do?"

As crappy as it all may seem, you can and you will get through it. That's what adulting is all about!

Fill in an adulting problem you're currently facing and then think about how Phoebe would handle it. Do you agree? Would you do the same?

What's On Your Mind?

_____

_____

_____

_____

_____

_____

_____

_____

_____

What Would Phoebe Do?

_____

_____

_____

_____

_____

_____

_____

_____

THE ONE
------ WITH ------
THE LIST

Life is never easy, and unfortunately having to make a big decision can make your life seem that much worse. This can range from "guac or no guac" (two dollars extra is something to ponder, buddy, don't you forget it!) to breakups and job offers.

Although Ross kind of blew it with his pros-and-cons list, it may not have been such a horrible idea on Chandler's part.

GAINING SOME CLARITY BEFORE SORTING OUT AN ISSUE IN YOUR OWN LIFE CAN REALLY EASE YOUR STRESS, SO IF YOU HAVE ANY IMPORTANT DECISIONS TO MAKE, TRY OUT THE SAME PROS-AND-CONS TECHNIQUE THAT ROSS USED WITH THE LIST HERE!

WHAT'S YOUR CONFLICT?

_____

_____

_____

PROS   CONS

_____

_____

_____

_____

_____

WHAT'S THE RESOLUTION?

_____

_____

_____

_____

_____

Whether your brother stares at your apartment from across the street (weird, Ross) or your two sisters only stop by every few Thanksgivings or so when they want something from you (best sibs ever!), your siblings are your family, and you should learn to engage with them like the adulty-dult you are.

This may mean anything from bonding over an old choreographed dance routine, standing up for your sister when your best friend insults them, or merely offering your bratty sib a bit of advice from time to time. Might as well—you were once a brat too.

Forming an adult relationship with your sibling(s) certainly takes time (and strength), but eventually you'll get the hang of it. And, if you have an evil twin sister, well...good luck with that hot mess.

Advantages of siblings while adulting

✓ They'll always defend you, even if you are in the wrong.

✓ You'll have a shoulder to cry on.

✓ You get a built-in babysitter for your kids.

✓ You might find a soul mate in your sibling's best friend!

Disadvantages of siblings while adulting

✓ They will embarrass you with memories from your past as a fat kid.

✓ They might play the bagpipes at your wedding.

✓ A sibling could drunkenly reveal all of your secrets at any moment.

✓ They might date your friends.

GUIDE TO: SiBLiNGS

YOU can't just GIVE UP. IS THAT WHAT A DINOSAUR WOULD DO?

—JOEY TRIBBIANI

JOEY'S
CHECKLIST

Even if Joey may not be the most "adult" among the group of friends, he definitely has his own redeeming qualities and adulting life lessons to share. And, c'mon, his chick and duck parenting skills...bravo!

Check off each of the good and bad adulting qualities you exhibit in your own life. How alike or different are you from Joey?

GOOD ADULTING HABITS

☐ Solid sandwich maker

☐ Loyal friend

☐ Confident

☐ Sensitive

☐ Great pet owner

☐ Fantastic wingman

BAD ADULTING HABITS

☐ Mooch (do not count on Joey to complete your Venmo requests)

☐ Doesn't share food (not even one French fry)

☐ Serial dater

☐ Mr. Steal Your Girl

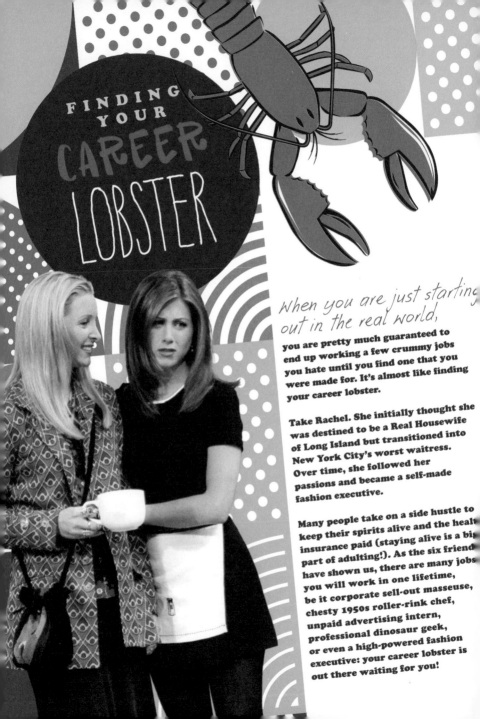

FINDING YOUR CAREER LOBSTER

When you are just starting out in the real world,

you are pretty much guaranteed to end up working a few crummy jobs you hate until you find one that you were made for. It's almost like finding your career lobster.

Take Rachel. She initially thought she was destined to be a Real Housewife of Long Island but transitioned into New York City's worst waitress. Over time, she followed her passions and became a self-made fashion executive.

Many people take on a side hustle to keep their spirits alive and the health insurance paid (staying alive is a big part of adulting!). As the six friends have shown us, there are many jobs you will work in one lifetime, be it corporate sell-out masseuse, chesty 1950s roller-rink chef, unpaid advertising intern, professional dinosaur geek, or even a high-powered fashion executive: your career lobster is out there waiting for you!

Which of the six friends do you think you would most like to work with for a day? Why?

_____

_____

_____

_____

_____

_____

_____

What was your dream job as a child?

_____

_____

_____

_____

_____

If you could pick any career in the world for yourself without limitations, what would it be?

_____

_____

_____

_____

_____

GUIDE TO:

HALLOWEEN

IT'S SAFE TO SAY THAT HALLOWEEN HAS THE POTENTIAL TO BE THE ULTIMATE HOLIDAY.

It's the chance to take a break from adulting for just a little while, throw on a cape, a mask, or a pink rabbit suit (it was either pink rabbit or no rabbit!), and pretend to be something that you absolutely positively are not.

If you decide to throw a Halloween party last minute, make sure you stick to the basics: stock up on enough ice, buy plenty of candy for the kids, avoid any and all adorable ballerinas, and, whatever you do, don't show up as Space Doody (it's a really bad look when you decide to arm wrestle the pink bunny).

BOO!

HALLOWEEN

Costume Ideas Inspired by the Friends!

✔ A Pregnant Woman "Who Spent A Lot Of Money On A Dress And She Wants To Wear It Because Soon She Won't Be Able To Fit Into It"

✔ Chandler

✔ Catwoman

✔ Supergirl

✔ Spud-nik

✔ Velveteen Rabbit

✔ Slutty Nurse

✔ The Solar System

✔ Charlie Brown

BOO!

BOO!

WHAT WOULD _____ Rachel _____ DO

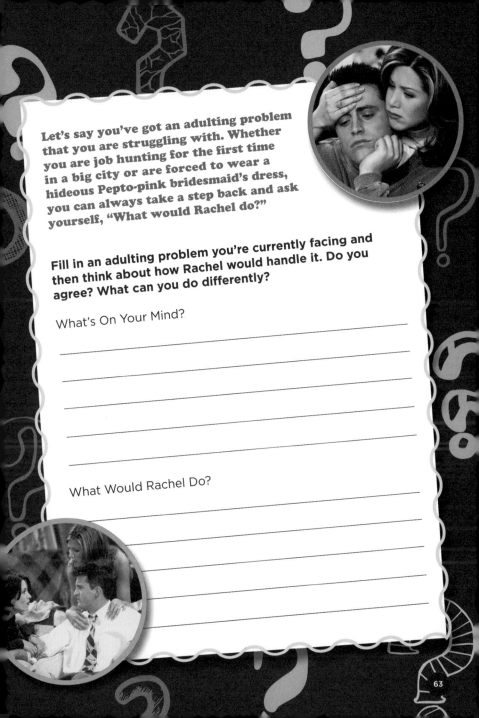

Let's say you've got an adulting problem that you are struggling with. Whether you are job hunting for the first time in a big city or are forced to wear a hideous Pepto-pink bridesmaid's dress, you can always take a step back and ask yourself, "What would Rachel do?"

Fill in an adulting problem you're currently facing and then think about how Rachel would handle it. Do you agree? What can you do differently?

What's On Your Mind?

_____

_____

_____

_____

_____

What Would Rachel Do?

_____

_____

_____

_____

_____

UNLIKE JOEY, YOU SHARE FOOD:

RACHEL'S

Ingredients:

1 package raspberries

1 jar raspberry jam

1 package ladyfing

3/4 cup peas

2 cups custard

1 banana

1/2 yellow onion

10 oz. ground beef

Whipped cream

TRIFLE

TRIFLE

Even though it might sound easier to throw a bucket of wings on the counter and call it done, a big part of getting older is helping out in the kitchen during the holidays. When Thanksgiving rolls around, this recipe will definitely come in handy when you are finally asked to prepare a dish for your holiday feast. Conveniently, this traditional English trifle appears to be a dessert and entrée all in one. Nothing says adulting more than multitasking!

The pressure is on, and not everyone can be a Monica in the kitchen, but you can damn sure try!

RECIPE

STEP ONE: Sauté ground beef with the peas and onions.

STEP TWO: Prepare the custard very carefully. Stir slowly as your friends watch in (fearful) anticipation.

STEP THREE: Line the bottom of a clear trifle bowl with a layer of those ladyfingers. Ask someone why they are called ladyfingers.

STEP FOUR: Hyperventilate.

STEP FIVE: Add a layer of raspberry jam until the lady fingers are completely covered. Then add a layer of custard and top with raspberries.

STEP SIX: Add another layer of ladyfingers. So many fingers.

STEP SEVEN: Add a layer of the beef mixture and then a layer of the rest of your custard and bananas. Repeat until your ingredients are all gone.

STEP EIGHT: Top your trifle with a heaping pile of whipped cream. Serve immediately. Watch your friends enjoy your delectable dessert far away from you in separate rooms!

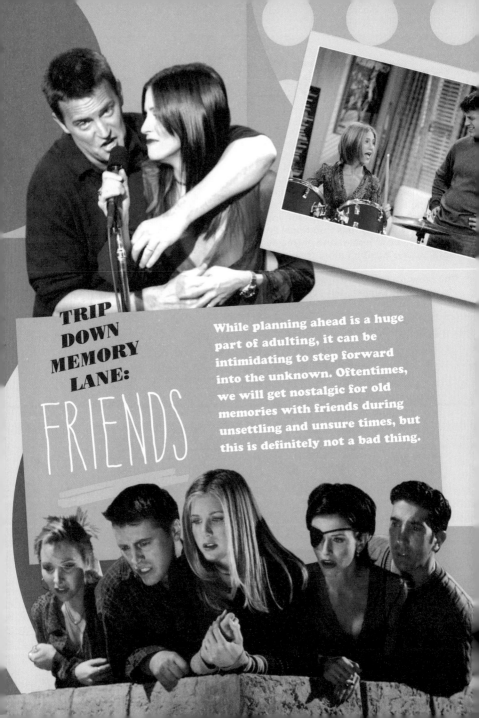

TRIP DOWN MEMORY LANE:
FRIENDS

While planning ahead is a huge part of adulting, it can be intimidating to step forward into the unknown. Oftentimes, we will get nostalgic for old memories with friends during unsettling and unsure times, but this is definitely not a bad thing.

Nostalgia can be an excellent stress coping mechanism.
**Take time to answer the questions below
and you'll see for yourself!**

Can you remember a time with your friends where you
laughed until you cried?

_____

_____

_____

_____

What other memories with friends bring you comfort in
times of uncertainty?

_____

_____

_____

_____

Don't think too hard! Who is the first friend you can
remember from childhood? What was the first memory
you had with them?

_____

_____

_____

_____

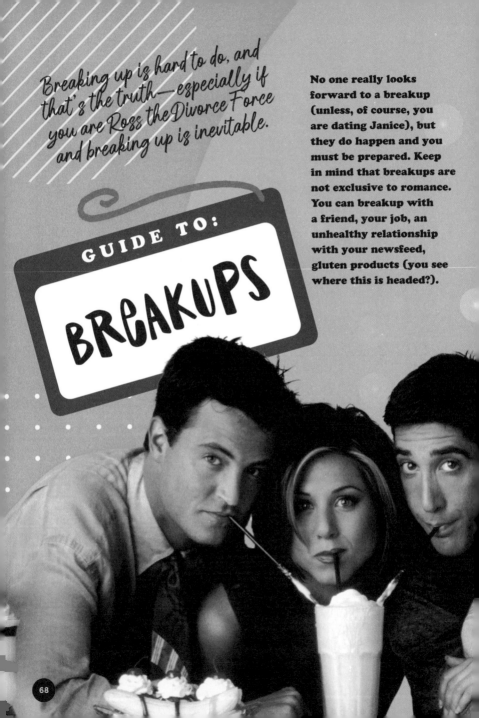

Breaking up is hard to do, and that's the truth—especially if you are Ross the Divorce Force and breaking up is inevitable.

GUIDE TO:
BREAKUPS

No one really looks forward to a breakup (unless, of course, you are dating Janice), but they do happen and you must be prepared. Keep in mind that breakups are not exclusive to romance. You can breakup with a friend, your job, an unhealthy relationship with your newsfeed, gluten products (you see where this is headed?).

Luckily, the six friends have lots of experience in the breakup department and can help you out through the many, many (but hopefully not too many) breakups you will experience throughout your life. So don't be too sad. There are many different fish (and gluten substitutes) in the sea. And just like the strong person you are, you will certainly be able to see this one through.

Breakup Dos and Don'ts

✓ Do define the terms of a break.

✓ Do be friends with an ex, if you are clear about expectations.

✓ Don't give ultimatums. It doesn't lead to healthy discussion.

✓ Don't repeat the same mistakes (seriously, Chandler).

ROSS'S
· GUIDE TO ·
aDULTiNG

1. Leather pants are never a good idea (and the combo of lotion and powder will only form a paste, which won't help pull the pants up).

2. Shell out the cash for movers to avoid any and all pivoting.

3. There is a difference between a break and a breakup.

4. Say the right name at the altar.

5. Take a deep, deep breath before charging at the man who ATE YOUR SANDWICH.

6. Don't give yourself a nickname, Red Ross!

7. Stick up for your sibling, even if you have a rivalry.

8. Never give up on true love.

9. If it doesn't work out, you can always get divorced.

10. Rent your Santa suit in advance so you don't end up as the Holiday Armadillo.

11. You must approach life like karate...with a total mastery of Unagi.

12. Let the technicalities go (even if you were on a break).

13. Fajitas can make any awkward situation a party.

14. Sometimes a secret language speaks louder than words.

15. Condoms are only 97% effective.

EVERYBODY LOOKS ~SO~ HAPPY. I HATE ...THAT.

—PHOEBE BUFFAY

For someone without a "pla," Phoebe Buffay is pretty much killing it. Sure, Phoebe didn't have an ideal childhood, but she certainly makes up for it with her badass adulting skills.

Check off each of the good and bad adulting qualities you exhibit in your own life. How alike or different are you from Phoebe?

GOOD ADULTING HABITS

- ☐ Resilient
- ☐ Open-minded
- ☐ Stays true to herself
- ☐ Street smart
- ☐ Has a side hustle/hustles
- ☐ Honest
- ☐ Confident
- ☐ Generous

BAD ADULTING HABITS

- ☐ Holds grudges
- ☐ Manipulative
- ☐ Bad secret keeper
- ☐ Has favorites (Joey)
- ☐ Hypocritical

PHOEBE'S CHECKLIST

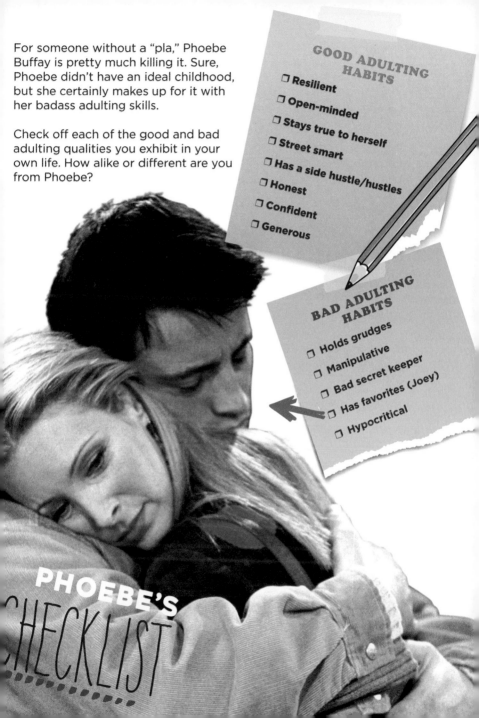

GUIDE TO: THANKSGIVING

Thanksgiving is, without a doubt, the holiday for making memories (and mashed potatoes three ways). Whether it's an ultra-competitive game of nose-breaking Thanksgiving football or an unexpected visit from your high-school hater, you are guaranteed to be entertained during Thanksgiving dinner.

Most importantly, Thanksgiving is a time to reflect on the things you are truly grateful for, so even if you hate Thanksgiving, or are spending it in a box this year, take a moment to say thanks: for your friends, your family, and for your toe—even if it's missing the tip!

THANKSGIVING TIPS
ACCORDING TO FRIENDS

Don't lie about a dog allergy.
Better yet, don't say you hate dogs.

FUNYUNS ARE THE ULTIMATE THANKSGIVING FOOD.

Fall in love with the girl who will stick
her head inside a turkey for you.

Don't bother using your wedding china
for literally anything.

NEVER BE LATE TO THANKSGIVING DINNER.

If you don't get along with your sister,
don't invite her to Thanksgiving.

If you pretend to watch the game,
you can get out of helping with dinner.

SOME PEOPLE SHOULD STAY OUT OF THE KITCHEN.

Always have a spare key to your apartment on hand.

Custard? Good. Meat? Good. Jam? Good.

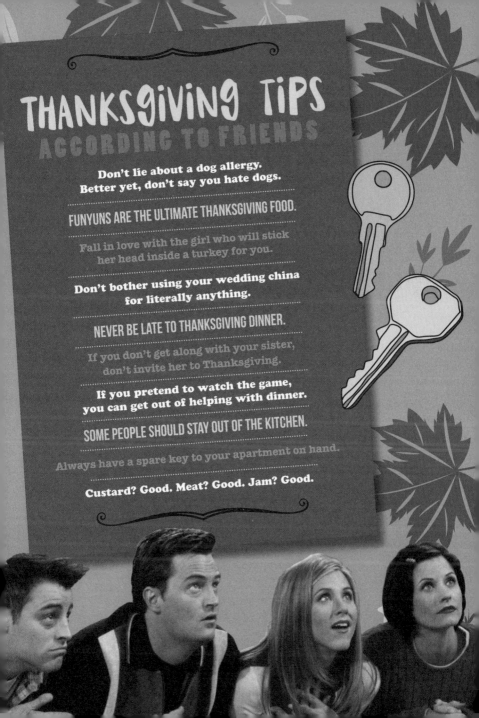

BIG BOOK OF GRIEVANCES: CAREER

GOT CAREER PROBLEMS?

Maybe everyone at work smokes—or vapes—at lunch and you are missing out on all the office gossip. Even worse, maybe your new coworker is a total robot (no, for real, his name is C.H.E.E.S.E.).

Like it or not, the little things add up, and sometimes you just need to let out your career complaints without consequences. Otherwise, you might go a little crazy.

Rather than explode like the delicious day—old curry that your coworker warmed up in the communal microwave for lunch, use the space below to air your grievances about work.

"I could so easily freak out right now."

UNLIKE JOEY, YOU SHARE FOOD:

THE MOISTMAKER SANDWICH

Put your adulting skills to the test and make use of your family dinner leftovers to create the ultimate Thanksgiving sandwich.

This recipe comes from the Geller family vault and is lovingly made by Monica every year. With a layer of gravy-soaked bread in between stuffing, turkey, cranberry sauce, and sandwich fixins, you are in for the ultimate post-Thanksgiving treat.

NOTE TO MOISTMAKER MAKER:

Protect your sandwich with your life, as word on the street is coworkers are often tempted by its Turkey Day perfection. If your sandwich is swiped, remain calm. Screaming at sandwich swipers won't end well for anyone.

The chance to make this delicious Thanksgiving leftovers sandwich comes around just once a year, so if you are going to steal the recipe from Ross, do him a favor and eat the whole dang sandwich.

GELLER FAMILY RECIPE

(YIELDS 4 MOISTMAKER SANDWICHES)

Ingredients

1 cup gravy
12 slices leftover turkey breast
12 slices sandwich bread, toasted
½ cup mayonnaise

8 slices lettuce
8 slices tomato
2 cups stuffing
1 cup cranberry sauce

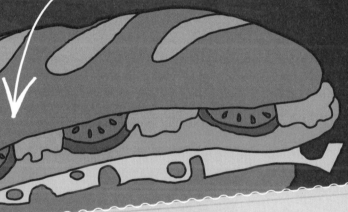

Instructions

1. Spread 1 tablespoon of mayonnaise on 2 slices of bread.

2. Top with two leaves of lettuce.

3. Add ½ cup of stuffing on top of the lettuce.

4. Place two slices of tomato on top of the stuffing.

5. Dip another slice of bread into the gravy and place on top of the tomato. This is the moistmaker.

6. Add 3 slices of leftover turkey breast.

7. Add ¼ cup cranberry sauce and top with a final piece of bread with the mayo. Voilà!

ONE thing is for sure: adulting is pretty

hard. And if anyone could agree with that statement it's Ross Geller.

Whether it's dealing with a big work project or the fact that you were on a break, when it comes down to it, your life choices are your own. That's kind of scary, but also pretty exciting!

"You're just jealous because you couldn't pull this off."

Fill in an adulting problem you're currently facing and then think about how Ross would handle it. Do you agree? What can you do differently?

What's On Your Mind?

_____

_____

_____

_____

_____

_____

_____

_____

What Would Ross Do?

_____

_____

_____

_____

_____

_____

_____

_____

_____

GUIDE TO:

DATING

IN TODAY'S WORLD OF SWIPE LEFT, DATING CAN BE PRETTY HARSH.

In fact, looking to the six friends, pretty much all of them experienced doubts, regrets, and anxiety toward dating, but they also had a lot of fun while playing the field too!

So step away from your matches and pay attention for a sec: You are going to fall on your face and go on some pretty awful dates. You may even have dinner with someone who will want to—gasp!—share your food. But relax, it is going to be okay. Eventually, you will find someone who you will totally vibe with, and you will look into your lobster's eyes and think, "Wow, dating was not great. I'm really glad that's over with!" Until then, be brave. You've totally got this.

"You've just gotta figure at some point it's all gonna come together."

Dating Dos and Don'ts

✔ Do put yourself out there, even if it is outside your comfort zone.

✔ Do play the field a little, even if it makes choosing a little bit harder. (You go, Pheebs.)

✔ Do be yourself.

✔ Don't let your baggage sour your relationships (*cough* Chandler).

✔ Don't confuse something physical for something emotional (talk about clingy, Ross!).

✔ Don't bring a date back without cleaning your apartment first!

THE ONE
------- WITH -------
THE LIST

Part of adulting includes making hefty, life-changing decisions (fun, right?). But decision-making can be kind of a waste without weighing the pros and cons. You cannot move forward without considering the consequences of your actions.

When Ross used a pros-and-cons list, it helped him clarify where he stood on his relationship with Rachel (even if it offended her in the long run).

If you have an important decision to make, try out the same pros-and-cons technique that Ross used with the list here! But be sure to keep this list to yourself! No one likes to read that they have chubby ankles.

WHAT'S YOUR CONFLICT?

_____

_____

_____

PROS

CONS

_____

_____

_____

_____

_____

WHAT'S THE RESOLUTION?

_____

_____

_____

_____

_____

WELCOME TO THE REAL WORLD. IT SUCKS. YOU'RE GONNA LOVE IT.

—MONICA GELLER

MONICA'S CHECKLIST

With her cleaning obsession and tightly wound personality, Monica definitely appears to have it all together on the adulting train, yet despite her pristine appearance, Monica still has some clutter in that closet.

Check off each of the good and bad adulting qualities you exhibit in your own life. How alike or different are you from Monica?

GOOD ADULTING HABITS

☐ Crazy neat (maybe a little too crazy...)

☐ Can cook a meal like nobody's business (avoid any and all delivery fees when Mon is around!)

☐ Ready and willing wedding planner (and rocks a headset and clipboard like a boss)

☐ World's greatest hostess (with the mostest)

☐ Total master of the glow-up

☐ Will take in a new roommate during her time of need

BAD ADULTING HABITS

☐ Control freak (no greasy fingers or tacky lamps allowed)

☐ Ultra competitive

☐ Secret hoarder (whatever you do, do not open that closet...)

☐ Will open wedding gifts without the groom present. (If you snooze you lose, right?)

☐ Will lie about her job for babies. (Call me Reverend Monica!)

HOLIDAYS

The holidays are a wonderful time of the year. 'Tis the season to spend with friends and family, be it caroling, baking, bickering, or opening presents.

Whether you put out cookies for Santa Claus, receive eight pairs of socks for Hanukkah (and delicious potato latkes!), or listen to life lessons from the Holiday Armadillo, this winter season can be an excellent time to put your adulting skills to the test. Maybe this is the year you will put out a holiday card with your significant other or ring a bell for the Salvation Army. As long as you are filled wit the holiday spirit, anything is possible!

PERFECT SECRET SANTA GIFT IDEAS ACCORDING TO THE FRIENDS

JOEY:
A sexy calendar (yes, they still exist) and two pizzas.

ROSS:
A subscription to Nat Geo.

CHANDLER:
A dumb joke book or a blind date!

MONICA:
A dry mop and a massage (not from Phoebe).

RACHEL:
A gift card (no one can pick a gift better than the recipient!).

PHOEBE:
A rescue puppy or a song!

Holiday If...Thens

IF you are late buying Christmas gifts... THEN stop off at the gas station for seat covers, air fresheners, soda pop, and condoms for all of your friends!

IF they run out of Santa suits... THEN bring in Santa's representative for all the Southern states and Mexico.

IF your S.O. wants to send out a holiday card... THEN give them a key to your apartment instead.

IF your friend is working at a Christmas tree lot... THEN convince them to save all the wimpy trees.

IF your friend leaves their apartment... THEN search for your Christmas presents.

PHOEBE'S
• GUIDE TO •
aDULTiNG

1. It's okay if you don't have a plan. It's even okay if you don't have a "pla."

2. The art of seduction is a great tool to have in your back pocket.

3. Don't be afraid to say "no" to the things you just don't want to do.

4. To express your feelings, write a song about it.

5. A second identity always comes in handy. (Hello, my name is Regina Phalange.)

6. Boyfriends and girlfriends will come and go, but friendship is for life.

7. The more you drink, the less there is for the kids to drink.

8. Santa pants make great maternity pants.

9. Always have faith in your talents.

10. When going for a jog, run like you are heading toward the swings or running away from Satan.

11. After the baby is born, maternity pants are great for shoplifting melons.

12. He may not be your soul mate, but a girl's gotta eat.

13. When someone compliments you, you should agree with them because it's true (obviously).

14. Don't hate. You don't want to put that out into the universe.

15. It's never too late to learn how to ride a bike.

HELLO
my name is
Regina
Phalange

TRIP DOWN MEMORY LANE:
FAMILY

Whether your parents have a favorite child, you and your brother have a strange choreographed dance routine, or your father has a secret mistress, all families have their issues, but that doesn't mean you can't look back on some memories with your family with fondness (or disdain—that's fine too).

"Get out and stop annoying me!"

Reflect on some of your favorite family memories below and take humor in the fact that every family member is a little bit funky.

Who is the strangest member of your family and why?

_____

_____

_____

_____

What is your favorite family memory or tradition?

_____

_____

_____

_____

Is there a member of your family you are closest to? Why do you think that is?

_____

_____

_____

In what ways do you remind yourself of your parents?

_____

_____

_____

_____

MONICA'S
· GUIDE TO ·
aDULTiNG

1. Do not let your competitive nature allow you to lose your apartment in a bet.

2. Shark porn isn't a thing.

3. A bad hair day can never bring a true winner down.

4. Have a type of towel on hand for every occasion—eleven kinds, to be precise.

5. If your boyfriend has the Thanksgiving blues, cheer him up with a dancing turkey.

6. It's okay to know you're really good at stuff.

7. Seven! SEVEN. Seven.

8. All rules are off when you are on London time.

9. Don't be afraid to tackle someone to get your dream wedding dress.

10. Give your expensive boots a good try before you buy: you can't return the boots once they are filled with your blood.

11. When your self-esteem is low, take an introductory class in something you are great at!

12. You can be harsh if someone is doing it wrong.

13. Even neat people have dirty secrets.

14. Don't count on your parents: they might use your wedding money to buy a beach house.

15. Leg wax can be an emergency snack in a pinch if you are stranded in your bedroom.

GUIDE TO: PARENTS

It's no secret that adulting can be difficult, but when you are dealing with crazy parents, it is especially important that your friends are there for you. Luckily, most people can relate.

Parents can be an excellent support system as you become your own adult, but they can also be a nightmare to deal with, especially if your mother is a best-selling erotic novelist with a book called *Mistress Bitch*, your rich father is a terrible tipper, or your mom cannot let go of the fat kid you once were.

A word of advice: parents are people too.

Just as you are learning to make mistakes in this time of your life, you must learn to compartmentalize. Approach your parents with love and understanding and realize that even parents have some growing up to do. And if you can't do that, squash your feelings down deep inside and take out your crazy on your own kids someday!

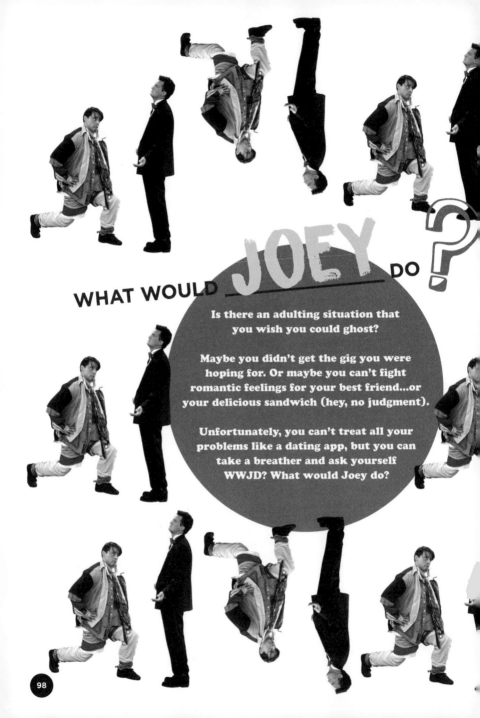

WHAT WOULD _____ JOEY DO ?

Is there an adulting situation that you wish you could ghost?

Maybe you didn't get the gig you were hoping for. Or maybe you can't fight romantic feelings for your best friend...or your delicious sandwich (hey, no judgment).

Unfortunately, you can't treat all your problems like a dating app, but you can take a breather and ask yourself WWJD? What would Joey do?

Fill in whatever problem you're facing and then think about how Joey would handle it. Do you agree? Would you do the same?

What's On Your Mind?

_____

_____

_____

_____

_____

_____

_____

_____

_____

What Would Joey Do?

_____

_____

_____

_____

_____

_____

_____

_____

_____

UNLIKE JOEY, YOU SHARE FOOD:

THE JOEY SPECIAL

Just as Thanksgiving isn't Thanksgiving without turkey, a Friday night isn't a Friday night without two pizzas. This is otherwise known as The Joey Special—a true adulting move because, hey, you're an adult & can have two pizzas if you want!

Not to get too cheesy here (and yes, pun fully intended), but pizza holds a very special place in all of our hearts. It's a reliable option after a long day at work, when cooking is completely out of the cards. You can count on pizza to be warm and inviting at any party and supportive during any and every sporting event. But most importantly, pizza is there for you the second you call and can be at your house in thirty minutes or less—talk about a true friend!

That's why it is essential to have the Joey Special pizza technique completely and fully mastered. You'll never know when it will come in handy. Who are you kidding? It will always come in handy.

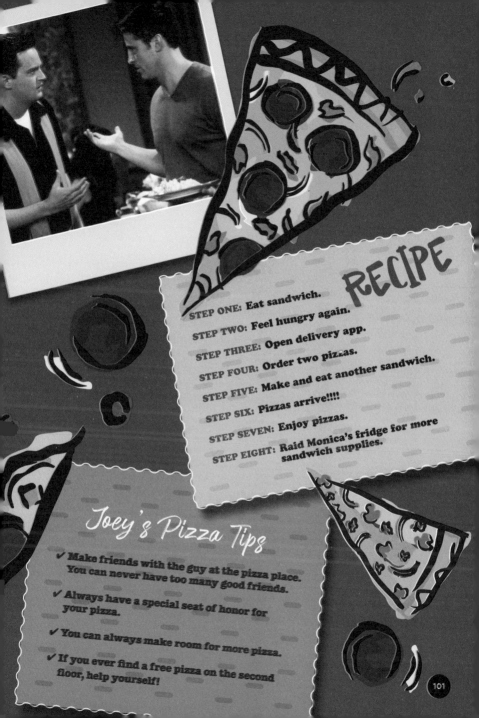

RECIPE

STEP ONE: Eat sandwich.

STEP TWO: Feel hungry again.

STEP THREE: Open delivery app.

STEP FOUR: Order two pizzas.

STEP FIVE: Make and eat another sandwich.

STEP SIX: Pizzas arrive!!!!

STEP SEVEN: Enjoy pizzas.

STEP EIGHT: Raid Monica's fridge for more sandwich supplies.

Joey's Pizza Tips

✓ Make friends with the guy at the pizza place. You can never have too many good friends.

✓ Always have a special seat of honor for your pizza.

✓ You can always make room for more pizza.

✓ If you ever find a free pizza on the second floor, help yourself!

UNTIL I WAS 25, I THOUGHT THE RESPONSE TO 'I LOVE YOU' WAS 'OH, CRAP.'

—CHANDLER BING

CHANDLER'S CHECKLIST

Chandler may have a stable job, but sometimes life isn't all it's cracked up to be (with the exception of a few sarcastic jokes). Nonetheless, Chandler manages to demonstrate some redeeming and not-so-redeeming traits as he figures out his own path.

Check off each of the good and bad adulting qualities you exhibit in your own life. How alike or different are you from Chandler?

BAD ADULTING HABITS

- ☐ Major mommy and daddy issues
- ☐ Commitment-phobe
- ☐ Bad dancer
- ☐ Won't know which of your sisters he kissed
- ☐ Sleeps during important work meetings

GOOD ADULTING HABITS

- ☐ Would lend money to a friend
- ☐ Super saver
- ☐ Can always break the tension with a joke
- ☐ Accepting of everyone's flaws
- ☐ Career oriented

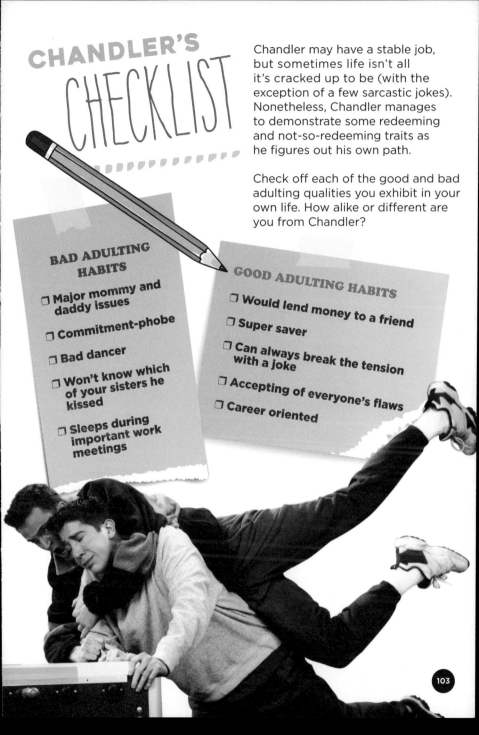

GUIDE TO:

CLEANING

Whether you are a total neat freak or the closest thing to cleaning in your apartment is throwing wet paper towels on the wall, keeping a tidy home is essential to maintaining yourself and your dwelling place.

There may be chores around the house that you never even learned to do because it was always done for you, or you may not do many chores because you don't really want to, but maintaining a clean living space is the first step to healthy and happy living! Besides, isn't it about time that you learned to do this stuff anyway, you filthy animal?

This doesn't mean you have to demand that there be a coaster on every surface and that people eat over their plates like Monica Geller, but you can take a few additional steps to maintain a clean living space. And with your surroundings clean, then you can really focus in on the hot mess that is yourself!

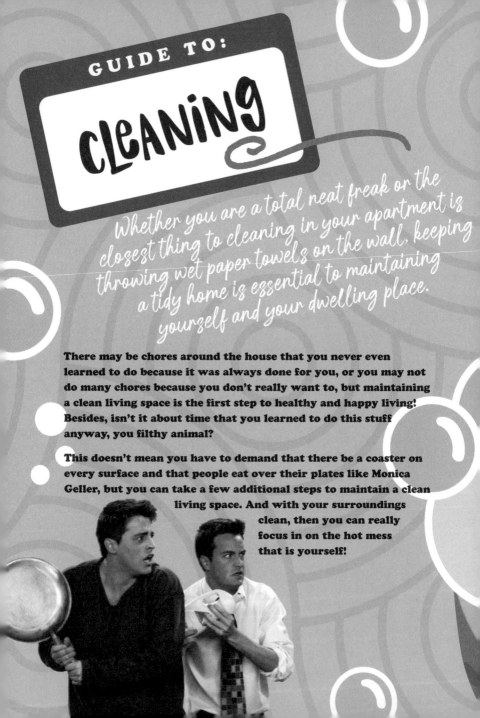

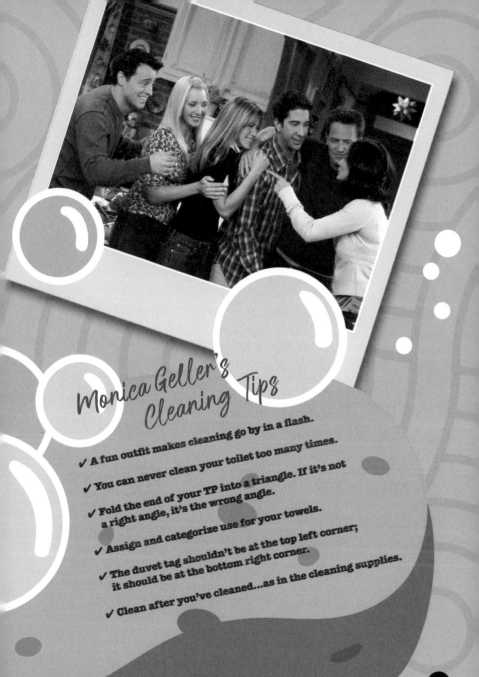

Monica Geller's Cleaning Tips

✓ A fun outfit makes cleaning go by in a flash.

✓ You can never clean your toilet too many times.

✓ Fold the end of your TP into a triangle. If it's not a right angle, it's the wrong angle.

✓ Assign and categorize use for your towels.

✓ The duvet tag shouldn't be at the top left corner; it should be at the bottom right corner.

✓ Clean after you've cleaned...as in the cleaning supplies.

CHANDLER'S
• GUIDE TO •
aDULTiNG

1. If you aren't good at advice, offer a sarcastic comment.

2. Don't lend a friend money and expect to be paid back.

3. If you're uncomfortable, make jokes.

4. Take the gum from the pretty lady in the ATM vestibule—it's perfection.

5. Don't let anyone talk you into wearing a thong if you don't want to.

6. Develop a "work laugh" to get through the workday or work party.

7. Don't sleep through a work meeting; you may volunteer to move to Tulsa, Oklahoma.

8. Bubble baths are highly underrated.

9. If you're engaged to a girl like Monica, be prepared to get a stand-in for your engagement photos.

10. Don't kiss your best friend's sister...unless she's the one you are going to marry.

11. Dance like nobody's watching because chances are everybody will be watching.

12. Test your dress shoes out before your wedding day.

13. Marry your best friend.

14. It is never too late to quit a job you hate.

15. You have to stop the Q-tip when there is resistance.

16. If you choose to play video games all day, be sure to take a stretch break (or four).

17. Never help your best friend move his couch.

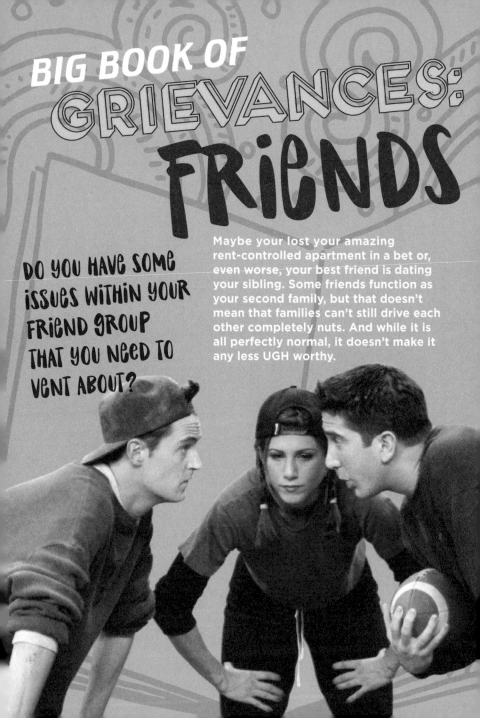

BIG BOOK OF GRIEVANCES: FRIENDS

DO YOU HAVE SOME ISSUES WITHIN YOUR FRIEND GROUP THAT YOU NEED TO VENT ABOUT?

Maybe your lost your amazing rent-controlled apartment in a bet or, even worse, your best friend is dating your sibling. Some friends function as your second family, but that doesn't mean that families can't still drive each other completely nuts. And while it is all perfectly normal, it doesn't make it any less UGH worthy.

Take the space below to air your grievances (like Chandler and Heckles!). What is bothering you right now about your friends?

_____

_____

_____

_____

_____

_____

_____

_____

_____

_____

_____

_____

_____

_____

_____

_____

_____

_____

GUIDE TO:

REUNIONS

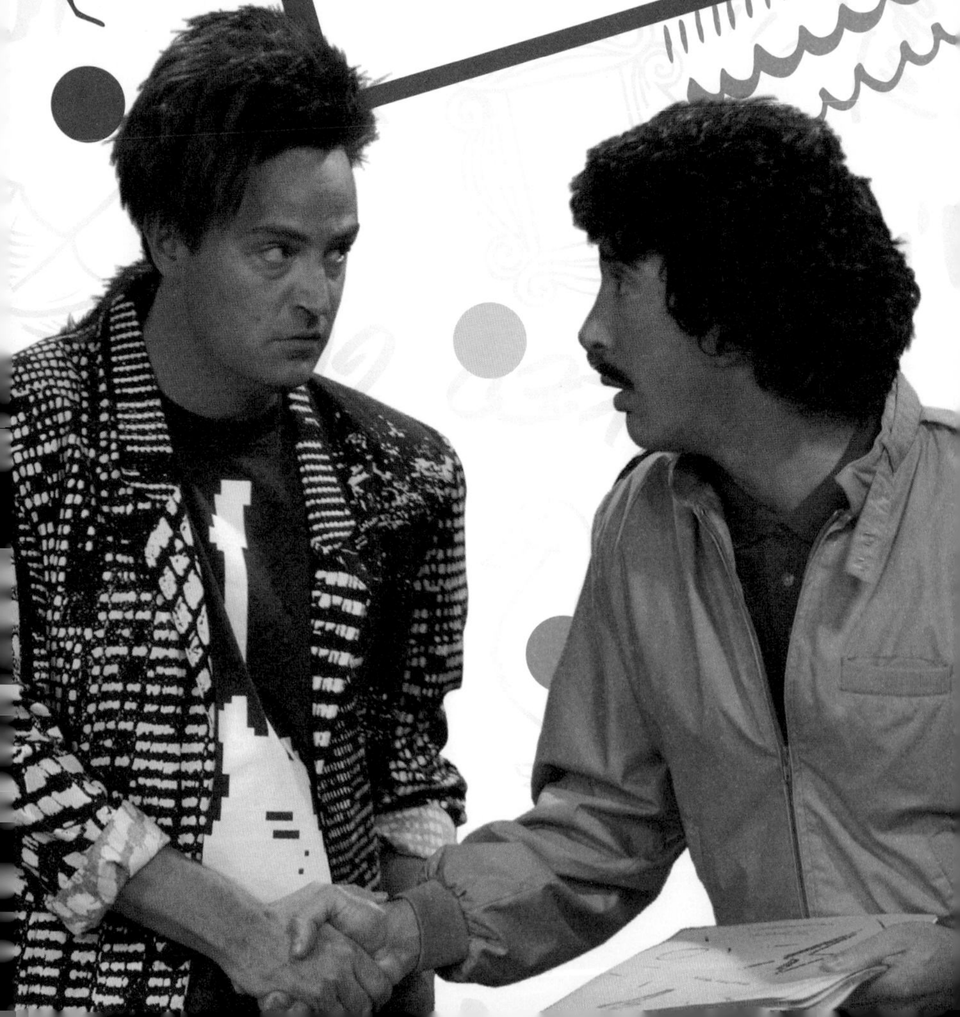

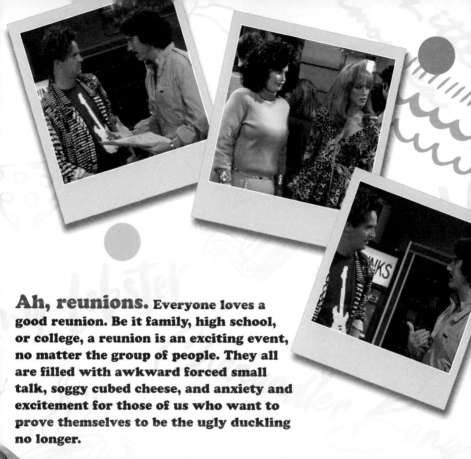

Ah, reunions. Everyone loves a good reunion. Be it family, high school, or college, a reunion is an exciting event, no matter the group of people. They all are filled with awkward forced small talk, soggy cubed cheese, and anxiety and excitement for those of us who want to prove themselves to be the ugly duckling no longer.

Remember when Ross and Chandler head to their college reunion? Their visit proved that a simple reunion with old classmates can uncover ghosts of our past, answering questions we were wondering about after all these years, and revealing other stuff that is better left a distant memory.

If you're headed to a reunion anytime ever, know that your past is in the past and your future is looking mighty bright. That is, of course, if you realize that your passionate first kiss was with your sister. Then, you may just need a few hefty rounds of therapy.

SEND-OFF

Now that you totally know how to adult,
get out there and do some adulting.
Good luck, friend!